Going to Grandma's

For Barry—my very own Travelin' Bear!—P. H.

LITTLE SIMON
An imprint of Simon & Schuster Children's Publishing Division
1230 Avenue of the Americas
New York, New York 10020

Library of Congress Cataloging-in-Publication Data
Hall, Patricia.
Going to Grandma's / by Patricia Hall ; illustrated by Kathryn Mitter.— 1st ed.
p. cm. — (Classic Raggedy Ann & Andy) (Ready-to-read)
Summary: When Raggedy Ann and Andy accompany Marcella on an airplane trip to visit her grandmother,
they are placed in the baggage compartment, where they play with a teddy bear they meet.
ISBN 0-689-84702-5 (alk. paper)
[1. Dolls—Fiction. 2. Air travel—Fiction. 3. Airplanes—Fiction. 4. Teddy bears—Fiction. 5. Toys—Fiction.] I.
Mitter, Kathy, ill. II. Title. III. Series. IV. Series: Ready-to-read
PZ7.H147515 Go 2001
[E]—dc21
2001029451

CLASSIC

Raggedy Ann & Andy

Going to Grandma's

by Patricia Hall
illustrated by Kathryn Mitter

Ready-to-Read

Little Simon

New York London Toronto Sydney Singapore

"We are going to Grandma's!"

Marcella said to Raggedy Ann and Andy.

"It is our first plane ride."

"You can ride inside my suitcase

for now.

When we get on the plane

you can come out to play," said Marcella.

 5

Marcella's suitcase did not fit

in its space on the plane.

"Your suitcase is **too** big!"

said the flight attendant.

"But do not worry!

We will put it

with the other suitcases

under the plane.

It was time for take-off.

Marcella buckled her seat belt.

"I am going to Grandma's!" she said.

She was very excited.

"Everything is so small!" said Marcella.

"Is that my house?"

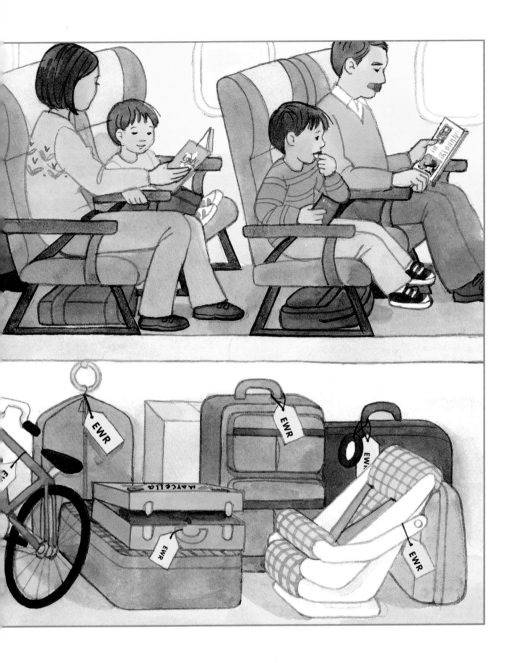

Marcella was having a lot of fun.

She did not miss her dolls.

"Time to play!" said Raggedy Andy.

They stepped out of the suitcase.

"**This** is not on the plane!"

said Raggedy Ann.

"Where are we?"

asked the Raggedys.

"You are in the **bottom** of the plane,"

said a voice.

A fuzzy, brown bear peeked out

 14

at the Raggedys.

"Hello! I am Travelin' Bear!

Who are you?"

"We are Raggedy Ann and

Raggedy Andy," said the dolls.

"We live with Marcella,

and we are going to Grandma's!"

said Raggedy Andy.

"Where do you live?"

asked Raggedy Ann.

"I live on this airplane!"

said Travelin Bear.

"I will show you around!"

said Travelin' Bear.

"Let's go!"

First he showed the Raggedys

how to swing.

Next he showed them

how to slide.

"I **love** to fly!" said Travelin' Bear.

"Whee!" giggled the Raggedys.

"**We** love to fly too!"

"You can stay with me

on the plane," said Travelin' Bear.

"We would have lots of fun!"

"No, thank you,"

said Raggedy Ann.

"We would miss Marcella."

"And," said Raggedy Andy,

"we are going to Grandma's!"

The airplane slowed down.

"Buckle your seat belts!" said the pilot.

"The airplane is landing!"

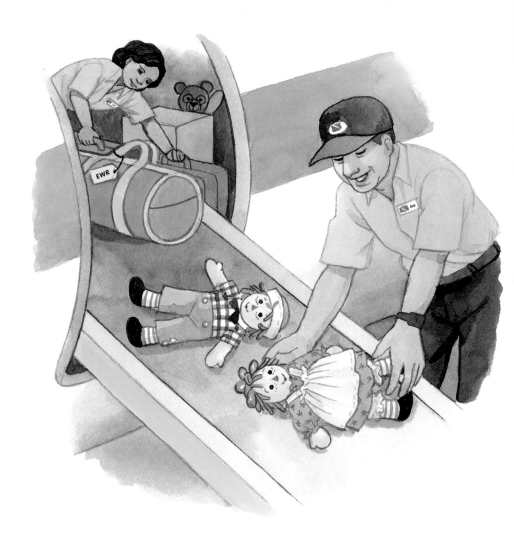

A nice man unloaded the suitcases.

"Look who I found!" he laughed.

He picked up the rag dolls.

Marcella's grandma met her

at the airport.

Marcella was happy to see her.

She told Grandma all about her trip.

Then Marcella remembered

the Raggedys!

"Are these dolls yours?"

the nice man asked.

"Raggedy Ann! Raggedy Andy!"

cried Marcella.

"I am so glad to see you!"

"I am sorry you fell out of my suitcase,"

Marcella said.

"I hope you did not miss me."

Raggedy Ann and Andy

just smiled.

Because everyone knows

that rag dolls do not talk!